ALICE in WONDERLAND

by Lewis Carroll
adapted by Mallory Loehr
illustrated by John Tenniel

A STEPPING STONE BOOK™
Random House 🏠 New York

❧   ❧   ❧

Published in the United States by Random House Children's Books, a division of Random House, Inc., New York. Random House and the colophon are registered trademarks and A Stepping Stone Book and the colophon are trademarks of Random House, Inc.

Visit us on the Web!
www.steppingstonesbooks.com
www.randomhouse.com/kids

Educators and librarians, for a variety of teaching tools, visit us at
www.randomhouse.com/teachers

Library of Congress Cataloging-in-Publication Data
Loehr, Mallory.
Alice in Wonderland / by Lewis Carroll ; adapted by Mallory Loehr ;
illustrated by John Tenniel. — 1st ed.
p.   cm.
"A Stepping Stone Book."
Summary: A shortened, simplified version of the tale in which a little girl falls down a rabbit hole and discovers a world of nonsensical and amusing characters.
ISBN 978-0-375-86641-8 (pbk.) — ISBN 978-0-375-96641-5 (lib. bdg.)
[1. Fantasy.] I. Tenniel, John, Sir, 1820–1914, ill. II. Carroll, Lewis, 1832–1898. Alice's adventures in Wonderland. III. Title.
PZ7.L82615Al 2009   [Fic]—dc22   2009018968

Printed in the United States of America   10 9 8 7 6 5 4 3 2 1

CONTENTS

CHAPTER ONE

Down the Rabbit Hole

Alice had nothing to do. She and her big sister were sitting on a riverbank. Her sister was reading a book with no pictures. It looked very boring.

Alice was thinking about making a daisy chain when a white rabbit ran by.

"Oh dear! Oh dear! I shall be too late!" the rabbit said. Then the rabbit took a watch out of his vest pocket. He looked at it and hurried on.

Alice jumped up and ran across the field

after the rabbit. The rabbit popped down a large rabbit hole under a hedge. Alice popped down after him.

The rabbit hole went along like a tunnel for some time. Then suddenly it dipped. Alice didn't have a moment to stop before she was falling down what seemed to be a well.

Either the well was very deep or Alice fell very slowly, for she had plenty of time to look around. Along the walls were bookshelves and cupboards. Maps and pictures hung on pegs.

Down, down, down. Would the fall never end? "I wonder how many miles I've fallen," Alice said. She tried to figure it out based on what she had learned in school about the size of the earth. Finally Alice gave up. The numbers were too big.

Down, down, down. There was nothing else

to do, so Alice began talking out loud. She pretended she was talking to her cat, Dinah. Then she just started to make up silly things.

"Do cats eat bats? Do bats eat cats?" she said. "Dinah, did you ever eat a bat?"

Suddenly, *thump, thump!* Alice landed on a heap of sticks and dry leaves. She was not a bit hurt.

She jumped up and looked around. She saw the White Rabbit, running down another long tunnel. He was quite far away. Alice ran like the wind to catch up with him.

"Oh my ears and whiskers, it's getting late!" he said. Then he dashed around a corner.

When Alice turned the corner, there was no sign of him. She was in a long, low hall. It was lit by a row of lamps hanging from the ceiling.

There were doors all around the hall. Alice

went up and down, trying all the doors. Every one was locked. Finally she stood in the middle of the hall. How was she ever going to get out again?

She noticed a three-legged table. It was made of solid glass. On top of it was a tiny golden key. Maybe the key belonged to one of the doors!

Alice tried the key in each of the doors. But either the locks were too large or the key was too small, for the key wouldn't open any of them.

However, Alice didn't give up and went past the doors again. This time she found a low curtain she hadn't seen before. Behind the curtain was a little door, only fifteen inches high. She tried the golden key in the lock. It fit!

Alice opened the door. It led to a small passage not much larger than a rat hole. She knelt down and looked along the passage. There at the end was the loveliest garden she'd ever seen! It had pretty fountains and rows of bright flowers.

Alice longed to go out of the dark hall and into the garden. But she could not get even her head through the door.

And even if I could get my head through, then what about my shoulders? Alice thought. *Oh, if only I could make myself close up like a telescope. I wonder how I could do it.*

You see, so many strange things had happened to Alice now that she thought anything was possible.

Alice wandered back to the table. She hoped she would find another tiny key . . . or a book about closing up like a telescope.

This time a little bottle stood on the table. A label was tied around the bottle's neck. On it were the words "DRINK ME" in large letters.

Well, Alice was not going to do *that* in a hurry.

"No, I'll look and see if it is marked 'poison,' " Alice said to herself. She knew terrible things happened to children who did not

follow simple rules. She was sure that if you drank from a bottle marked "poison," sooner or later it was going to make you sick.

The bottle was not marked "poison." So Alice tasted it. It tasted very nice, like a mix of cherry tart, custard, pineapple, roast turkey, toffee, and buttered toast. Alice quickly finished it off.

"What a curious feeling," said Alice. "I must be closing up like a telescope."

And so she was. Alice was now only ten inches tall—just the right size for the door to the garden! She ran to the door, but it was locked.

The golden key was back on the table. Alice could plainly see it through the glass top, now far above her. Alice tried to climb a table leg, but it was too slippery. She tried and tried, until she was too tired to try anymore.

Then she sat down and cried.

When she stopped crying, she looked around again. A little glass box lay under the table. Alice opened the box. Inside was a very small cake. The words "EAT ME" were written in raisins on the top.

"I'll eat it," said Alice. "If it makes me grow larger, I can reach the key. If it makes me grow smaller, I can creep under the door. Either way, I'll get into the garden. And I don't care which happens."

She ate a little bit. Then she held her hand over her head and said, "Which way? Which way?" To her surprise, she stayed the same size.

So she ate up the rest of the cake.

CHAPTER TWO

The Pool of Tears

"Curiouser and curiouser!" cried Alice. "I am opening up like the biggest telescope ever! Good-bye, feet!" She said this because when she looked down at her feet, they seemed very far away.

Alice kept growing until her head hit the ceiling. She was now more than nine feet high. She took the golden key from the glass table and ran to the garden door.

Poor Alice! There was no way she was going to get through the door. She could only see the garden by lying on her side and looking through the door with one eye.

She was mad at herself for crying, but she couldn't help it. She wept gallons of tears. She stopped at last when she heard little footsteps.

Alice dried her tears quickly. She was lying in a puddle of tears four inches deep. The footsteps belonged to the rabbit.

He was now quite dressed up. He had a pair of gloves in one hand and a large fan in the other. As he ran, he talked to himself. "Oh, the duchess, the duchess. She will be angry if I am late!" he said.

Alice felt quite desperate, so she spoke to the rabbit. "If you please, sir . . . ," she began in a low, timid voice.

The rabbit started. Then he dropped the

gloves and the fan and ran away as fast as he could.

Alice picked up the fan and gloves. The hall was very hot, so she fanned herself. She kept fanning until she looked down at her hands. She saw that she had put on one of the White Rabbit's gloves.

"I must be growing small again!" she said to herself.

Alice went back to the table to measure herself. It seemed she was about two feet tall and getting smaller. Maybe it was the fan that was making her shrink. She dropped it just in time to save herself from shrinking away completely.

"That was a narrow escape!" Alice said. "And now for the garden!"

But the garden door was locked again, and the key still on the table.

"Things are worse than ever!" she said. "I was never this small, never!"

As Alice spoke these words, her foot slipped. In another moment, *splash!* She was up to her chin in salt water.

Her first thought was, *I've fallen into the sea!* Then she remembered her tears. It wasn't the sea at all. It was a pool of her own tears. "I wish I hadn't cried so much!" she said.

As Alice tried to find her way out of the pool of tears, she heard a loud splashing a little way off. She swam nearer, thinking it must be a walrus or a hippopotamus. It was a mouse.

"Do you know the way out of this pool?" Alice asked.

The mouse just looked at her. Maybe it didn't understand English. So she tried talking in French. But the only thing she knew how to say in French was "Where is the cat?" So that is what she said.

The mouse leaped out of the water in fright.

"Oh, I beg your pardon!" cried Alice. "I forgot that mice don't like cats!"

"Not like cats!" cried the mouse, quivering

all over. "Would *you* like cats if you were me?"

"Perhaps not," said Alice. "But I think you would like Dinah, if you knew her."

The mouse glared at her.

"How about dogs?" Alice tried. "There is a nice little dog that lives nearby."

The mouse started swimming away.

"Mouse, dear," Alice called, "do come back. I won't talk about cats or dogs!"

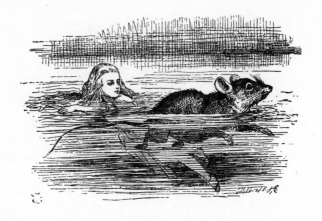

When the mouse heard this, it turned around. "Let us get to shore, then," it said to Alice.

By now the pool was getting quite crowded. Swimming about were a duck, a dodo, an eaglet, and many other creatures. Alice led the way, and the whole party swam to shore.

Once they were out of the water, the animals talked about how to get dry. Finally the mouse said that he would tell them a story that would surely dry them off. All the animals were quiet.

Then the mouse told them a long and very boring story about politics.

"It is not drying me at all," Alice said in the middle of the story. "I am as wet as ever."

Everyone agreed with Alice, so the mouse stopped his story. The dodo suggested racing until they dried off. Around and around the animals and Alice ran until the dodo declared the race was over. The dodo was right. They were all dry.

Someone asked the dodo who had won. He thought for a while, then said, "Everyone has won, and all must have prizes."

"But who is going to give the prizes?" the animals asked.

"Why, she, of course," said the dodo, pointing to Alice.

The animals crowded around Alice. "Prizes! Prizes!" they all called.

Alice dug into her pocket and pulled out a box of candy. Luckily, there was one piece for each winner.

But what about Alice? The mouse said that she should have a prize as well. So Alice found a thimble in her pocket. She gave it to the dodo.

"We beg you to accept this humble thimble," the dodo said to Alice. He gave her back her thimble.

Alice thought it was all very silly, as indeed it was.

Then all the animals hurried off to their homes.

Alice was left alone. She wondered how she was ever going to get back to *her* home. She was about to cry again when she heard the patter of little feet.

CHAPTER THREE

The Rabbit Sends In Little Bill

It was the White Rabbit. He was walking back and forth as if he was searching for something.

"Oh my paws and whiskers," he said. "The duchess will have my head! Where can I have dropped them?"

Alice knew that the rabbit must be hunting for his gloves and fan. She looked around for them. Everything seemed to have changed after her swim in the pool. The great hall with the door and the glass table had vanished.

Soon the rabbit saw Alice. "Why, Mary Ann, what are you doing here?" he asked. "Run home and fetch me a pair of gloves and a fan! Quick, now!"

Alice was so frightened, she ran off at once in the direction the rabbit pointed. "He doesn't know who I am," she said to herself. "But I'd better take him his fan and gloves—if I can find them."

As she said this, she came upon a neat little house. On a brass plate were the words "W. RABBIT." Alice walked in without knocking and went upstairs to hunt for the gloves and fan. She hoped she would not run into the real Mary Ann.

Alice found her way to a tidy room. There

was a table at a window. A fan and three pairs of tiny white gloves lay on the table.

Alice picked up the fan and one pair of gloves. Then she saw a little bottle near the looking glass. There was no label on it, but Alice decided to drink it anyway.

"Something interesting happens whenever I eat or drink anything here," she said to herself. "I do hope I grow again!"

Before Alice had drunk half the bottle, she felt her head pressing against the ceiling.

"That is quite enough," she said, putting the bottle down. "I wish I hadn't drunk so much!"

But Alice went on growing and growing and growing. She barely fit in the little room anymore. Finally she had to stick one foot up the chimney and one arm out the window. It was very uncomfortable.

"I can't do any more than this," Alice said. "I wonder what will become of me now."

Luckily for Alice, the magic was done and she stopped growing. But she was stuck.

It is much nicer at home, Alice thought. *Where I am not always growing and shrinking and being ordered about by mice and rabbits. When I used to read fairy tales, I thought none of it was true. Now here I am in the middle of one! There ought to be a book written about me. When I grow up, I'll write one.*

Alice kept thinking things like this until she heard a voice outside.

"Mary Ann! Mary Ann!" said the rabbit. "Fetch me my gloves this moment!"

There came a pattering of little feet on the stairs. Then the rabbit pushed against the door to the room. But it wouldn't open because Alice's giant elbow was pressed against it.

"I'll go around and get in the window," the rabbit said.

That you won't! Alice thought.

Alice waited until she believed she heard the rabbit under the window. Then she spread out her hand and made a snatch in the air. She didn't catch anything. But there was a little scream and the sound of breaking glass.

"Pat! Pat! Where are you?" came the rabbit's angry voice. "Come and help me!"

There were sounds of more broken glass.
Then the rabbit said, "Now tell me, Pat,
what's that in the window?"

"It's an arm," said a new voice.

That must be Pat, thought Alice.

"An arm, you goose!" said the rabbit. "Who ever saw one that size? It fills the window!"

"Sure it does," said Pat. "But for all that, it's still an arm."

"Well, it has no business being here!" said the rabbit. "Take it away."

Alice heard a lot of whispering. She spread out her hand and snatched the air again. This time there were two little shrieks and even more breaking glass.

Alice waited some time without hearing anything. At last came a rumbling like cart wheels and the sound of many voices talking. Alice tried to hear what they were saying.

She made out the words: "Where's the other ladder?" "Why, Bill's got it!" "Bill, put it here!" "Tie them together." "That's it!" "Oh, it's coming down!" "Someone's got to go down the chimney." "Bill's got to go down!" "Here, Bill! Master says you have to go down the chimney."

Poor Bill, thought Alice. Even so, she knew she had to do something. She drew her foot down the chimney as far as she could and waited. When she heard a scratching about in the chimney, she gave a sharp kick.

"There goes Bill!" came a chorus of voices from outside.

Then the voices talked about what to do next. After a minute or two, Alice heard the creatures outside moving. A shower of pebbles rattled through the window.

"You'd better not do that again!" Alice yelled. Instant silence fell.

Alice was surprised to see that the pebbles on the floor were all turning into little cakes.

If I eat one of the cakes, I will grow bigger or smaller, Alice thought. *And since I can't get any bigger, then I'll have to get smaller.*

So she swallowed one of the cakes. Right away she began shrinking. When Alice was small enough to fit through the door, she ran out of the house.

A crowd of small animals and birds stood around a lizard. *That must be Bill,* Alice thought.

The creatures saw Alice, and all made a rush at her. She ran off as fast as she could, and soon found herself safe in a thick wood.

"The first thing I've got to do," Alice said to herself, "is grow to my right size. And the second thing I've got to do is find my way into that lovely garden."

It was all very well to have such a plan, but carrying it out was another thing altogether. Alice wandered about the wood, looking for the right thing to eat or drink. Finally she came upon a large mushroom, about her height.

Alice looked under the mushroom and on both sides of it. Then she stretched up on tiptoe and peeped over the top. Her eyes met those of a large blue caterpillar.

CHAPTER FOUR

The Advice
from a Caterpillar

The Caterpillar and Alice looked at each other.

The Caterpillar had its arms folded. It was smoking a long pipe called a hookah. Finally it took the hookah out of its mouth and spoke.

"Who are you?" the Caterpillar asked.

"I hardly know," Alice said. "I knew when I woke up this morning. But I have changed so many times since then, I can't possibly be the same."

"Explain yourself," said the Caterpillar.

"I can't explain myself," said Alice, "because I am not myself, you see."

"I don't see," said the Caterpillar.

"I don't understand it, either," Alice said. "Being many different sizes in a day is confusing."

"It isn't," said the Caterpillar.

"Maybe you don't think so yet," Alice replied. "But once you make a cocoon and become a butterfly, you might think differently."

"No," said the Caterpillar. "I won't."

Alice was starting to find the Caterpillar annoying, and she turned away.

"Come back!" said the Caterpillar. "I have something important to say."

This sounded promising to Alice. She turned around again.

"Keep your temper," said the Caterpillar.

"Is that all?" Alice asked, trying to keep her temper.

"No," said the Caterpillar.

Alice folded her arms and waited.

"What size would you like to be?" asked the Caterpillar.

"I should like to be a little larger," said Alice. "Three inches is much too small."

"It is a very good height indeed," said the Caterpillar angrily, stretching up to its full length, which was exactly three inches.

"But I am not used to it!" Alice cried. She wished the creatures in this place didn't get upset so easily.

"You'll get used to it," the Caterpillar said. It yawned and shook itself. Then it got down from the mushroom.

"One side will make you grow taller. The

other side will make you grow shorter," the
Caterpillar said, crawling into the grass.

One side of what? The other side of what? thought
Alice.

"Of the mushroom," said the Caterpillar, as

if Alice had spoken out loud. In another moment, it was gone.

Alice looked at the mushroom, trying to figure out the two sides of it. Did a round mushroom *have* two sides? Finally she put her arms around it as far as they would go and broke off a bit of the edge with each hand.

"And now which is which?" she asked herself.

Alice nibbled a bit of mushroom from the right hand. She started shrinking. Right away she nibbled a bit of mushroom from the left hand, and grew. She went on nibbling back and forth until she was her normal size.

It felt quite strange at first, but she got used to it quickly. She began walking through the woods again.

"There's half my plan done," Alice said as

she walked. "Now for the second half. All I have to do is get into the beautiful garden. I wonder how I shall find it."

Just after she said this, she came to an open place in the woods. In it was a little house about four feet tall.

"It will never do to meet whoever lives there while I am this height," Alice said. "It would frighten them way too much."

Alice went back into the woods. She still had the two pieces of mushroom in her hands. So she nibbled from each again until she was nine inches high. She put what was left of the mushroom pieces into her pocket.

Alice peeked around the trees at the little house. While she was wondering what to do next, a fish dressed in a coat and hat and wig rushed out of the woods. He went and rapped

on the door of the house. A dressed-up frog
in a wig answered the door.

Alice crept a little way out of the woods to
see what was happening.

The fish pulled out a giant letter. It was nearly
as big as he was. He handed it to the frog.

"For the duchess," the fish said. "It is an

invitation to play croquet with the queen."

"For the duchess," the frog repeated. "An invitation to play croquet with the queen."

Then both the fish and the frog bowed low. The curls on their wigs got tangled together. They struggled to get apart.

At this, Alice began laughing. She laughed so hard that she had to run back into the woods so the fish and the frog wouldn't hear her. When she next peeped out, the fish was gone. The frog sat on the ground, staring at the sky.

Alice went to the door and knocked.

"There is no use knocking, for two reasons," said the frog. "One, I am on the same side of the door as you. And two, because it is so loud inside, no one could possibly hear you."

Alice listened. The frog was right. From

inside the house came a lot of noise. It sounded like howling and sneezing at the same time. And every few minutes came a terrific crash, as if something had been broken into pieces.

"Please, then," said Alice, "how am I to get in?"

Just then the door opened, and a large plate sailed out. It grazed the frog's nose and broke on a tree behind him.

"I shall sit here," said the frog, "on and off for days and days."

"That's all very well," said Alice, "but what am I to do?"

"Anything you like," said the frog. He began whistling.

"Oh, there's no use talking to him," Alice said to herself. And she opened the door and went in.

CHAPTER FIVE

Pig and Pepper

The door led right into a large kitchen. It was full of smoke.

The duchess was sitting on a stool in the middle, holding a baby. The cook was leaning over the fire, stirring a pot. Alice thought the pot must hold soup.

Alice began to sneeze. *There is too much pepper in that soup!* she thought.

There was certainly too much pepper in the air. The baby sneezed and howled. The duchess sneezed. Alice sneezed. Only the cook and a cat sitting near the fire didn't sneeze.

The cat was grinning from ear to ear.

"Please, will you tell me why your cat grins like that?" Alice asked.

"It's a Cheshire Cat," said the duchess. "And that's why. Pig!" She said this last word so loudly that Alice jumped.

Alice saw that the duchess was not speaking to her, but to the baby. "I didn't know Cheshire Cats always grinned," Alice said. "In fact, I didn't know that cats *could* grin."

"They all can, and some do," said the duchess.

"I don't know of any who do," said Alice. She was quite pleased to be having a real conversation with someone.

"You don't know much," said the duchess. "And that's a fact."

Alice decided to change the subject, while

the cook decided to throw everything she could at the duchess and the baby. The duchess took no notice of the pots and pans and dishes flying past. The baby howled.

One large pan sailed by the baby's nose. "Oh, do be careful!" Alice cried to the cook.

But the cook was back to stirring the pot as if nothing had happened.

"Here, you can hold the baby," said the

duchess. She tossed the baby to Alice. "I must get ready to play croquet with the queen."

Alice barely caught the baby.

The duchess ran out of the room. The cook threw a frying pan after her and just missed.

In Alice's arms, the baby began sneezing and snorting. Alice thought it best to go outside.

"It is not safe here at all," she said, heading into the open air.

The baby grunted, as if it agreed. Alice looked into its face to see if something was wrong. She saw that the baby had a very turned-up nose.

It is more like a snout than a nose, thought Alice. *And its eyes seem very small. Maybe that is from crying so much.* She looked closely at the baby's little eyes. There were no tears.

"If you are going to turn into a pig, I'll have

nothing more to do with you," Alice told the baby.

The baby grunted again. Alice looked down. There was no doubt about it. The baby was a pig.

"It's no use carrying a pig about," said Alice. So she put the pig down, and it ran into the woods.

"It would have been an ugly child," Alice said to herself. "But it is a rather handsome pig."

She was startled to see the Cheshire Cat sitting in a tree a few yards off. The cat grinned at her. Alice thought it seemed friendly.

"Cheshire Cat, would you please tell me which way I should go from here?" Alice asked as politely as she could.

"That depends on where you want to get to," said the cat.

"I don't much care—" Alice began.

"Then it doesn't matter which way you go," said the cat.

"—so long as I get *somewhere*," Alice finished.

"Oh, you're sure to do that," said the cat, "if you only walk long enough."

Alice thought this was clear, so she asked, "What sort of people live around here?"

The cat waved his right paw. "The hatter lives that way." The cat waved his left paw. "And the March Hare lives that way. Visit either one. They are both mad."

"But I don't want to visit mad people," said Alice.

"Oh, you can't help that," said the cat. "We're all mad here. I'm mad. You're mad."

"How do you know I'm mad?" asked Alice.

"You must be," said the cat. "Or you wouldn't have come here."

Alice didn't think this made sense, but she went on. "How do you know that *you're* mad?" she asked.

"To begin with, a dog is not mad," said the cat. "Do you agree?"

"I suppose so," said Alice.

"A dog growls when it is angry and wags its tail when it is happy," said the cat. "I growl when I am happy and wag my tail when I am angry. Therefore, I am mad."

"*I* call it purring, not growling," said Alice.

"Call it what you like," said the cat. "Are

you playing croquet with the queen today?"

"I would like to," said Alice. "But I haven't been invited."

"You'll see me there," said the cat, and it vanished.

Alice was not surprised. She was getting used to things being strange. She was still looking at the spot where the cat had been when it appeared again.

"What happened to the baby?" the cat asked.

"It turned into a pig," said Alice.

"I thought it would," said the cat, and it vanished again.

Alice waited to see if it would come back. When it didn't, she walked off in the direction of the March Hare.

"I've seen hatters before," she said to herself. "The March Hare will be more interesting.

And since it is May, maybe the hare won't be so mad."

As she said this, she noticed the cat was back.

"Did you say 'pig' or 'fig'?" the cat asked.

"Pig," said Alice. "And I wish you wouldn't come and go so suddenly. It is making me giddy."

"All right," said the cat. This time it vanished slowly. It started with its tail and ended with its grin. The grin stayed a long time after the rest of it had gone.

CHAPTER SIX

A Mad Tea Party

There was a table set out under a tree in front of the March Hare's house. The March Hare and the Mad Hatter were having tea. A dormouse sat between them. It was fast asleep.

The table was large, but the hare, the hatter, and the Dormouse were crowded together.

"No room! No room!" cried the hare and the hatter when they saw Alice.

"There's *plenty* of room!" Alice said. She sat down in an armchair at one end of the table.

"It isn't polite of you to sit without asking," said the March Hare.

"I didn't know it was your table," said Alice.

"Your hair wants cutting," said the hatter.

"That is a rude thing to say," Alice replied.

The hatter opened his eyes wide. "Why is a raven like a writing desk?" he asked.

Alice was glad they'd come to riddles. They'd have some fun now! "I can guess that, I think," Alice said.

"Do you mean that you think you can find out the answer to it?" asked the March Hare.

"Exactly," said Alice.

"Then you should say what you mean," said the hare.

"I do," said Alice. "At least I mean what I say. That's the same thing."

"Not at all," declared the hatter. "You might as well say 'I see what I eat' is the same as 'I eat what I see.' "

"You might as well say 'I like what I get' is the same as 'I get what I like,' " said the hare.

"You might as well say," added the Dormouse, talking in his sleep, "that 'I breathe when I sleep' is the same as 'I sleep when I breathe.' "

"It is the same thing for you," the hatter said to the Dormouse.

At this, everyone fell silent. Alice thought about what she could remember about ravens and writing desks.

The Mad Hatter broke the silence. "What day of the month is it?" he asked. He took his watch out of his pocket and looked at it.

"The fourth," said Alice.

"Two days wrong," sighed the hatter, shaking his watch. "I told you butter isn't good for watches," he said to the hare.

"It was the *best* butter," said the hare.

"Yes, but crumbs must have got in," said the hatter. He dipped the watch into his cup of tea.

Alice looked at him curiously. "What a funny watch!" she said. "It tells the month and day, but not the time."

"Why should it?" asked the hatter. "Does your watch tell the year?"

"No," said Alice. "But that's because it stays the same year for so long."

"Just the same as mine," said the hatter.

Alice was utterly confused.

"Have you guessed the riddle yet?" the hatter asked.

"No, I give up," Alice replied. "What is the answer?"

"I haven't the slightest idea," said the hatter.

"Nor I," said the March Hare.

"It is a waste of time asking riddles with no answers," Alice snapped.

"Time won't do a thing I ask," said the hatter. "It is always six o'clock."

This made no sense to Alice, but it did give her a thought. "Is that why there are so many tea things on the table?"

"Yes," said the hatter. "It's always teatime. There's never any time to wash the things in between."

"So you keep moving around?" Alice said.

"Exactly," said the hatter. "As the things get used up."

"Suppose the young lady tells us a story," the March Hare suggested, changing the subject.

"I'm afraid I don't know one," said Alice.

"Then the Dormouse shall!" said the hatter and the hare together. They pinched the poor Dormouse on both sides.

The Dormouse opened its eyes. "I wasn't asleep," it said. "I heard everything."

"Tell us a story!" ordered the March Hare.

"Once upon a time, there were three sisters," began the Dormouse. "They lived in a well."

"What did they eat?" Alice asked. She was always interested in what people ate and drank.

The Dormouse thought for a minute. "Treacle."

Alice was quite concerned. The three sisters would have been very ill. Treacle was quite sweet, like syrup.

"Take some more tea," the March Hare said to Alice.

"But I haven't had *any* tea," Alice pointed out. "So I can't take *more* tea."

"You mean you can't take *less*," said the hatter. "It's easy to take *more* than nothing."

Alice didn't know what to say to this, so she

helped herself to tea and bread-and-butter. Then she turned to the Dormouse and asked, "Why did they live at the bottom of the well?"

The Dormouse took another minute to think. "It was a treacle well," it said.

"There's no such thing," Alice said.

"If you can't be nice, then *you* can finish the story," said the Dormouse. But then it went on. "The sisters were learning to draw—"

"Draw what?" Alice interrupted.

"Treacle," said the Dormouse, quickly this time.

"I want a clean cup," said the hatter. "Let's all move one place on."

The Mad Hatter moved. The Dormouse moved into the hatter's place. The March Hare moved into the Dormouse's place. Alice moved into the March Hare's place. Alice was a good deal worse off. Her cup was dirty, and the March Hare had spilled milk on his plate.

"I don't understand," Alice said to the Dormouse. "Where did the sisters draw the treacle?"

"You can draw water from a well," said the Dormouse. "So you can draw treacle from a treacle well."

"But they were *in* the well!" Alice protested.

"Of course they were," said the Dormouse. "*Well* in."

Now Alice was really confused. "I don't think—" she began.

"Then you shouldn't speak," snapped the Mad Hatter.

This was more than Alice could bear. She got up from the table and walked off.

Alice looked back a few times. She half

hoped the hatter and the hare would call her
back. The last time she looked around, they were
trying to stuff the Dormouse into a teapot.

"I'll never go there again," said Alice, walking through the woods. "It was the stupidest
tea party I ever went to in my life."

She kept walking until she saw a door in
one of the trees.

"That's curious," Alice said to herself. "But everything is curious today. I might as well go in at once." And in she went.

Once more Alice was in the long hall with the little glass table. *I'll get it right this time,* she thought.

Alice took the golden key and unlocked the garden door. Then she took the mushroom pieces out of her pocket. She nibbled from each until she was a foot high.

Alice passed through the door. At last she was in the beautiful garden!

CHAPTER SEVEN

The Queen's Croquet Party

A rose tree stood near the entrance of the garden. The roses on it were white, but three gardeners were painting them red. Alice went closer to watch. The gardeners were flat rectangles with hands and feet at the corners.

"Look here, Five," one of the gardeners said. "Don't go splashing paint on me."

"Seven jogged my elbow!" said Five.

"That's right," said Seven. "Blame someone else."

"You shouldn't talk," said Five. "Yesterday the queen said you should be beheaded."

"What for?" asked the first gardener.

"None of your business, Two," said Seven.

"He brought the cook tulip roots instead of onions," said Five.

Seven flung down his brush and opened his mouth to say something. At that moment, he saw Alice. He closed his mouth tight.

The two other gardeners looked around and saw Alice, too. Then all three of them bowed low.

"Why are you painting the roses?" Alice asked.

"The fact is, this was supposed to be a red rose tree," Two said. "We put in a white one by mistake. If the queen finds out, we shall all have our heads cut off. So—"

"The queen! The queen!" called Five.

The gardeners threw themselves flat on their faces. There was the sound of many footsteps. Alice looked around.

First came ten soldiers carrying clubs. They were shaped like the gardeners. Then came ten lords covered with diamonds. After these came the ten royal children, who ran and jumped about happily.

Next came the guests, mostly kings and queens. Alice saw the White Rabbit, but he didn't notice her. He was followed by the Knave of Hearts. Last came the King and Queen of Hearts.

The procession stopped when it reached Alice.

"Who is this?" the queen asked the knave.

He bowed and smiled.

"Idiot!" said the queen. "What is your name?" she asked Alice.

"Alice," said Alice. She added quietly to herself, "Why, they're only a pack of cards. I needn't be afraid of them."

"And who are these?" the queen asked, pointing to the gardeners.

"How should I know?" said Alice. "It is none of my business."

The queen turned red with fury. "Off with her head!" she screamed. "Off with—"

"Nonsense!" said Alice loudly.

"She's only a child, my dear," the king said to the queen.

The queen glared at him. She turned to the knave. "Turn them over!" she said.

The knave turned the gardeners over with one foot.

"Get up!" yelled the queen in a shrill voice.

The gardeners leaped up and began bowing.

"Stop!" shouted the queen. "You're making me dizzy!" She looked at the rose tree. "What have you been doing?"

"May it please Your Majesty," said Two, "we were trying—"

"I see!" said the queen, who had been studying the roses. "Off with their heads!"

The procession moved on, except for three soldiers who stayed to chop off the heads of the gardeners. The gardeners ran behind Alice.

"You won't be beheaded," Alice told them.

She put the gardeners into a large flowerpot. The soldiers wandered about for a minute or two. Then they marched off after the others.

"Are their heads off?" shouted the queen.

"Their heads are gone!" said the soldiers.

"Can you play croquet?" shouted the queen.

The soldiers looked at Alice.

"Yes!" shouted Alice.

"Come on, then," roared the queen.

So Alice joined the procession.

"It's a very fine day," came a small voice at Alice's side. It was the White Rabbit.

"Very," said Alice. "Where is the duchess?"

"Hush," said the rabbit. He looked over his shoulder. Then he went on tiptoe and whispered into Alice's ear, "She's to be beheaded."

"What for?" asked Alice.

"She boxed the queen's ears," said the rabbit.

Alice laughed out loud.

"Hush!" said the rabbit. "The queen will hear you! The queen will—"

"Get to your places!" shouted the queen in a voice like thunder.

People ran in all directions. Alice went to join them. Finally everyone got sorted out and the game began.

It was the strangest croquet game Alice had ever seen. The balls were live hedgehogs. The mallets were live flamingos. The arches were soldiers bent in half.

Every time Alice got her flamingo to straighten its neck so she could hit the hedge-hog ball, it turned to look at her. The flamingo seemed so puzzled that Alice kept laughing. By the time Alice stopped and had the flamingo ready again, the hedgehog had unrolled itself.

To make it even
harder, the soldier
arches kept moving
to new spots on
the field. Everyone
played at once, with-
out waiting turns.
The players fought
with each other and
for the hedgehog balls. It didn't take long for
the queen to start shouting "Off with his
head!" and "Off with her head!"

Alice was feeling very uneasy. She hadn't
fought much with the queen yet, but she knew
it could happen any minute. *They are very fond of*
beheading people here, Alice thought. *It is a wonder*
there's anyone left!

She was looking around for a way to escape when she noticed a curious thing in the air. She kept looking and saw that it was a grin slowly appearing.

"It's the Cheshire Cat!" Alice said.

"How are you getting on?" asked the cat as soon as there was enough grin to speak.

Alice waited for the eyes to appear. Then she nodded. *It's no use speaking until its ears have appeared,* she thought.

In another minute, the cat's whole head was hanging in the air.

"They fight so loudly," Alice complained to the cat. "And there are no rules, or at least no one follows them. It's very confusing."

"How do you like the queen?" asked the cat's head. No more of its body had appeared.

"Not at all," said Alice. "She's so very"—Alice saw that the queen was right behind her and listening, so she went on—"likely to win that it is hardly worth playing."

The queen smiled and passed on.

"Who are you talking to?" asked the king. He looked at the cat's head with great interest.

"It's a friend of mine," said Alice. "The Cheshire Cat."

"I don't like the look of it at all," said the king. "But it can kiss my hand if it likes."

"I'd rather not," said the cat.

"Don't look at me like that!" said the king.

"A cat may look at a king," said Alice. "I read that somewhere."

"Well, it must be taken away," said the king. He called to the queen, "My dear! You must have this cat taken away!"

The queen had a solution for settling all problems. "Off with its head!" she shouted, without even turning around.

"I'll get a soldier," said the king, and he hurried off to find one.

The queen then screamed for three players to be beheaded for missing their turns. Alice quickly went to find her hedgehog before she was next.

CHAPTER EIGHT

The Griffin
and the Mock Turtle

Alice found her hedgehog, but now her
flamingo had gone to the other side of the
garden. By the time Alice got to the flamingo,
her hedgehog was out of sight. So Alice went
back to the Cheshire Cat.

A large crowd stood around the cat's head
now.

The king, the queen, and a soldier were
arguing loudly. The soldier pointed out that
you couldn't behead something without a

body. The king said anything with a head could be beheaded. And the queen said if the matter was not taken care of right away, she'd have *everyone* beheaded.

"You should talk to the duchess," said Alice. "It's her cat."

"Fetch the duchess!" screamed the queen.

The soldier went off like an arrow. As soon as he was gone, the Cheshire Cat's head began fading away. By the time the soldier returned with the duchess, the cat had completely vanished.

The king and the soldier ran around looking for it. Everyone else went back to the game.

The duchess took Alice's arm. "It's so good to see you again," said the duchess.

Alice was happy to see the duchess in such a good mood. *Maybe all she needed was to be away from the pepper,* Alice thought.

The duchess went on talking, but Alice wasn't listening. Instead, she was wondering about things like pepper making people angry and what makes the world go around. When Alice felt the duchess's arm shake, she looked up.

The queen was standing in front of them,

her face like a thundercloud. She glared at the duchess. "Either you or your head must be off," the Queen of Hearts shouted, stamping her foot. "Take your choice."

The duchess took her choice and was gone in a moment.

"Back to the game!" the queen said to Alice.

Too scared to say a word, Alice slowly followed the queen.

The other players jumped up from where they had been resting, and the game went on. The queen never once stopped fighting or shouting "Off with his head!" and "Off with her head!"

At the end of half an hour, there were no players left except the queen, the king, and Alice. And the arches were all gone, since the soldiers had to take the other players away.

With just the three of them, the queen finally stopped yelling. She turned to Alice and asked, "Have you seen the Mock Turtle yet?"

"No," said Alice. "I don't even know what a mock turtle is."

"It's what mock turtle soup is made from," the queen told her.

"I never saw or heard of one," said Alice.

"Come on, then," said the queen.

As they walked off, Alice heard the king say, "Everyone will be pardoned and go free." This made her feel much better.

Alice and the queen soon came upon a griffin lying fast asleep in the sun. (If you don't know what a griffin is, look at the picture on page 82.)

"Up, griffin," said the queen. "And take this

young lady to the Mock Turtle to hear his story. I have some beheadings to see to." With that, the queen walked off.

Alice thought the griffin looked a bit scary. Then she thought that the queen *was* scary, so she was probably better off with the griffin.

The griffin sat up. It watched the queen until she was gone. Then it chuckled. "What fun!" said the griffin.

"*What* is the fun?" asked Alice.

"Why, *she*," said the griffin. "It's all her fancy. They never cut anyone's head off in the end, you know. Come on!"

I am so tired of always being told to "come on" by all the creatures here, Alice thought. But she followed the griffin until they came to the Mock Turtle.

"The queen wants you to tell this young lady your story," said the griffin.

"I will," said the Mock Turtle. "But don't say a word until I've finished."

Alice and the griffin sat. No one spoke. Not even the Mock Turtle.

How can he finish if he doesn't begin? thought Alice.

"Once," said the Mock Turtle at last, with a deep sigh, "I was a real turtle."

Then he began to sob. He sobbed for so long, Alice was about to get up. But she felt sure there was more to come.

"When I was little," the Mock Turtle finally said, "I went to school in the sea. The teacher was an old turtle. We called him Tortoise—"

"Why did you call him Tortoise if he wasn't one?" Alice asked.

"We called him Tortoise because he taught us, of course," said the turtle.

Then the griffin and the turtle stared at Alice until she wanted to sink into the earth. At last the griffin turned to the turtle and said, "Go on. Don't be all day about it!"

"I went to school in the sea," the turtle repeated. "The best education. School every day and—"

"*I've* been to a school every day, too," said Alice. "You needn't be so proud of it."

"With extras?" the Mock Turtle asked.

"Yes," said Alice. "French and music."

"And washing?" asked the Mock Turtle.

"Certainly not!" said Alice.

"Ah, then yours was not a really good school," said the Mock Turtle. "Now, ours had French and music *and* washing!"

"You couldn't have needed washing much in the sea," Alice pointed out.

"I didn't learn it, in any case," said the turtle sadly. "I only had time for Reeling and Writhing and Mystery lessons. Then there was Drawling."

"How many hours a day did you do lessons?" Alice asked.

"Ten hours the first day," said the turtle. "Nine the second day, and so on."

"What an odd way to do it," said Alice.

"That's why they are called lessons," said the griffin. "Because they *lessen* every day. But that's enough about lessons. Tell her something about the games."

The Mock Turtle sighed deeply. He wiped his eyes with a flipper and began to sob again. When he stopped, he said, sniffling, "You can have no idea what the Lobster Dance is."

"No indeed," said Alice. "What is it?"

"First you form a line," said the griffin.

"Two lines!" said the turtle. "Seals, turtles, and so on. Then you clear the jellyfish out of the way. You walk forward twice—"

"With a lobster partner!" cried the griffin. "Back and forth a few times, then change lobsters!"

"Then you throw the lobsters into the sea as far as you can!" shouted the Mock Turtle.

"And swim after them!" screamed the griffin.

"Turn a somersault in the sea!" cried the turtle, dancing wildly about.

"Change lobsters again!" yelled the griffin.

"Back to land and—that's the first part," said the Mock Turtle, suddenly dropping his voice.

The griffin and the turtle, who had been

jumping about like mad things, sat down quietly. They looked at Alice.

"It must be very pretty," said Alice.

"It is," said the griffin. "Now let's hear some
of your adventures."

"I could tell you about today," said Alice.
"But it's no use going back to yesterday. I was
a different person then."

"Explain," said the Mock Turtle.

"No, no! Adventures first!" said the griffin. "Explaining takes too long."

So Alice told them of her adventures, beginning with the White Rabbit. The two creatures listened with their eyes and mouths wide. They were perfectly silent until she got to the end.

"That's very curious," said the Mock Turtle.

Alice quite agreed.

Just then came a distant cry of "The trial's beginning!"

"Come on!" said the griffin, taking Alice by the hand.

"What trial is it?" asked Alice.

The griffin just repeated, "Come on!" Then he hurried Alice away.

CHAPTER NINE

Who Stole the Tarts?

The King and Queen of Hearts were on their thrones when Alice and the griffin got to the courtroom. A great crowd had gathered—birds and beasts as well as the whole pack of cards.

The Knave of Hearts stood in front of the king and queen. He was wrapped in chains.

Near the king was the White Rabbit. He had a trumpet in one hand and a large piece of paper rolled up in the other. In the middle of the court was a table. It had a big plate of tarts on it.

I wish they'd get the trial done and hand out the tarts,
Alice thought.

Alice had never been in a courtroom before,
but she had read about them.

"That's the judge," she said to herself, "because he has a wig on."

The judge was the king. He wore his crown
over his wig, which looked quite silly.

"And that's the jury," said Alice, seeing
twelve creatures grouped together in a box.

The twelve jurors were busy writing on slates.

"What are they writing?" Alice asked the
griffin. "The trial hasn't started yet."

"They are writing their names, in case they
forget them before the trial is over," said the
griffin.

"Stupid things!" Alice said loudly.

"Silence in the court!" cried the White Rabbit. The king put on his glasses and looked around to see who was talking.

All the jurors were writing down "stupid things" on their slates. One of them didn't even know how to spell "stupid."

A nice muddle their notes will be in before the trial is done, thought Alice.

"Read the charge," the king said.

The White Rabbit blew three times on his trumpet. Then he unrolled his piece of paper and read:

"The Queen of Hearts, she made some tarts,
All on a summer day.
The Knave of Hearts, he stole those tarts,
And took them quite away."

"Think about your verdict," the king told the jury.

"Not yet! Not yet!" the rabbit said. "There's a great deal more to come!"

"Call the first witness!" said the king.

The White Rabbit blew three more blasts on the trumpet. "First witness!" he called.

The first witness was the hatter. He came in with a teacup in one hand and a piece of bread-and-butter in the other. The March Hare followed him into the court, arm in arm with the Dormouse.

"I beg your pardon, Your Majesty, for bringing these in," the hatter said. "But I hadn't quite finished my tea when you called."

"You ought to have finished," said the king. "When did you begin?"

The hatter looked at the March Hare. "The

fourteenth of March, I *think* it was," said the hatter.

"Fifteenth," said the March Hare.

"Sixteenth," said the Dormouse.

"Write that down," the king told the jurors.

The jury all wrote on their slates.

"Take off your hat," the king said to the hatter.

"It isn't mine," said the hatter.

"Stolen!" the king said. He turned to the jury, who all wrote down "stolen" on their slates as if it were a fact.

"I keep them to sell," explained the hatter. "I don't own any of them. I'm a hatter!"

Here the queen put on her glasses. She stared hard at the hatter. The hatter turned pale and began to shake a bit.

"Give your evidence," said the king. "And

don't be nervous, or I'll have your head chopped off right away."

This did not make the hatter feel any better. He kept shifting from one foot to the other, looking uneasily at the queen. He took a bite out of his teacup instead of his bread-and-butter.

At this time, Alice began to feel very strange. It took her another moment before she realized that she was growing bigger again. She nearly got up to leave, then she decided to stay as long as there was room for her.

"I wish you wouldn't squeeze so," said the Dormouse. He was sitting next to Alice. "I can hardly breathe."

"I can't help it," Alice said. "I'm growing."

"You've no right to grow here," said the Dormouse.

"That's nonsense," Alice stated boldly.

"You know that you're growing, too."

"Yes, but *I* grow at a reasonable pace," said the Dormouse. He got up and went to the other side of the courtroom.

The queen had not stopped staring at the hatter. Just as the Dormouse crossed the court, she said, "Bring me the list of singers from the last concert." At this, the hatter shook so hard that both his shoes came off.

"Give your evidence!" the king repeated. "Or I will have your head chopped off, whether you are nervous or not!"

"I'm a poor man," the hatter began in a shaking voice. "And I hadn't started my tea— not more than a week or so—and what with the bread-and-butter getting so thin—and the twinkling of the tea—"

"The twinkling of the *what*?" asked the king.

"It *began* with the tea," said the hatter.

"Of course 'twinkling' *begins* with a 't,'" said the king sharply. "Do you take me for a dunce? Go on!"

"I'm a poor man," the hatter went on. "And

most things twinkled after that—only the March Hare said—"

"I didn't!" the March Hare interrupted in a great hurry.

"You did!" said the hatter.

"I deny it!" said the March Hare.

"He denies it," said the king. "Leave out that part."

"Well, at any rate, the Dormouse said . . ." The hatter looked around to see if the Dormouse would deny it.

The Dormouse didn't deny anything. He was fast asleep.

"After that," the hatter went on, "I cut some more bread-and-butter—"

"What did the Dormouse say?" one of the jurors asked.

"I can't remember," said the hatter.

"You *must* remember," said the king. "Or your head comes off!"

The unhappy hatter dropped his teacup and his bread-and-butter. He went down on one knee. "I'm a poor man, Your Majesty," he began again.

"You're a *very* poor *speaker!*" said the king. "If that is all you know about, you may stand down."

"I can't go any lower," said the hatter. "I am on the floor as it is."

"Then you may sit down," said the king.

"I'd rather finish my tea," said the hatter. He looked worriedly at the queen. She was reading the list of singers.

"You may go," said the king.

The hatter ran from the court. He didn't even put his shoes back on.

"Just take his head off outside," said the queen to one of the soldiers.

But the hatter was out of sight before the soldier could get to the door.

CHAPTER TEN

The Last Bit of Evidence

The next witness was the duchess's cook. She carried the pepperbox in her hand. Alice guessed what it was even before she saw it because everyone began sneezing.

"Give your evidence," said the king.

"No," said the cook.

The king looked at the White Rabbit.

"You must ask this witness *questions*," the White Rabbit said quietly to the king.

The king nodded unhappily. He folded his arms and frowned at the cook until his eyes nearly vanished. "What are tarts made of?" he asked in a deep voice.

"Pepper mostly," said the cook.

"Treacle," said a sleepy voice behind her.

"Get the Dormouse!" shouted the queen. "Behead him! Turn him out of the court! Silence him! Pinch him! Off with his whiskers!"

The whole court was thrown into a tizzy. Finally the Dormouse was carried out of the court. By the time everyone settled again, the cook was gone.

"Never mind," said the king, looking happier. "Call the next witness!" He added softly to the queen, "If the next one needs to be questioned, you must do it yourself. It makes my forehead ache."

Alice watched the White Rabbit as he

fumbled over the list. She was curious who would be next. *There hasn't been much in the way of evidence yet,* she thought.

Imagine her surprise when the White Rabbit said at the top of his shrill little voice, "Alice!"

"Here!" cried Alice, jumping up. She had grown so big in the last few minutes that she tipped over the jury box!

The jurors fell all over the place.

"Oh, I beg your pardon!" Alice said, and began picking them up as fast as she could.

Finally all the jurors were back where they belonged and the trial went on.

"What do you know about this business?" the king asked Alice.

"Nothing," said Alice.

"Nothing *whatever?*" asked the king.

"Nothing whatever," said Alice.

"That's very important," said the king to the jury.

The jury all began writing, then the White Rabbit said, "You mean *un*important, Your Majesty."

"*Un*important, of course, I meant," said the king. He began writing something down in his notebook.

The poor jurors

were confused as well. Half wrote "important" and half wrote "unimportant."

"Silence!" the king called. He read out from
his notebook, "Rule number forty-two. All
persons more than a mile high are to leave
the court."

Everybody looked at Alice.

"*I'm* not a mile high," said Alice.

"You are," said the king.

"Nearly two miles high!" said the queen.

"Well, I won't go," said Alice. "Besides,
that's not a regular rule. You just made it up!"

"It's the oldest rule in the book," said the king.

"Then it ought to be rule number one," said
Alice.

The king turned pale and shut his notebook
quickly.

"More evidence has just been found," said

the White Rabbit, holding up a piece of paper. "It seems to be a letter."

"Who is it to?" asked one of the jurors.

"There's nothing written on the outside," said the rabbit. He unfolded the paper. "It's not a letter. It's a poem."

"Is it in the prisoner's handwriting?" asked the king.

"No," said the White Rabbit.

"The knave must have written like someone else then," said the king.

"I didn't write it, Your Majesty," said the knave. "And you can't prove that I did."

"Read the poem," commanded the king.

The White Rabbit read the poem out loud. There were so many *him*s and *her*s and *he*s and *she*s that Alice's head was in a muddle.

Why, that poem makes no sense whatsoever, thought Alice. Although this didn't surprise her at all, given the whole adventure.

"This is the most important evidence so far," said the king, rubbing his hands together.

"If anyone can explain it," said Alice, "I'll give him sixpence. I don't believe there is an atom of meaning to it!" Alice was now so big that even the queen didn't scare her.

"Let the jury consider their verdict," the king said.

"No, no," said the queen. "Sentence first, verdict afterward."

"Stuff and nonsense!" said Alice loudly. "The idea of having the sentence first!"

"Hold your tongue!" said the queen, turning purple.

"I won't!" said Alice.

"Off with her head!" shouted the queen at the top of her voice.

Nobody moved.

"Who cares for you?" cried Alice. She had grown to her full size. "You're nothing but a pack of cards!"

At this, the whole pack rose up in the air and came flying down on her. Alice gave a little scream. When she tried to beat them off, she found herself lying on the riverbank. Her head was in her sister's lap. Her sister was gently brushing away some dead leaves that had fluttered down from the tree onto Alice's face.

"Wake up, Alice," said her sister. "What a long sleep you've had!"

"Oh, I've had such a curious dream!" said Alice. She told her sister as much as she could remember of all the adventures that you have been reading about.

"It *was* a curious dream," said her sister. "But now it is time to go in for tea. It's getting late."

Alice ran inside, but her sister stayed a moment more on the riverbank. She closed her eyes and imagined the White Rabbit running by and all the voices of the creatures and people Alice had dreamed about.

She thought of Alice growing up someday. She could imagine a grown-up Alice telling children her stories, maybe even the story of the Wonderland of today's dream. And in telling the stories, she knew Alice would remember her own childhood and these happy summer days.

About the Author

The oldest boy of eleven children, Charles Dodgson, who wrote under the name **Lewis Carroll**, was born in 1832 in Daresbury, England. While he was working at Oxford University, he became good friends with the Liddell family, and made up stories for the girls, Lorina, Alice, and Edith. *Alice's Adventures in Wonderland* grew out of one of those stories, which he first told to Alice and her sisters on a boat trip. It was published in 1865, and a sequel, *Through the Looking-Glass and What Alice Found There*, was published in 1871.

If you liked
Alice in Wonderland,
you won't want to miss these stories!

Mary Lennox has heard stories of a locked,
deserted garden somewhere on her
uncle's land. Will she be able to find
the magic of the secret garden?